The *Cam Jansen* Series

★

★

CAM JANSEN
and
the Mystery of
the U.F.O.

★ ★

DAVID A. ADLER
Illustrated by Susanna Natti

★ ★

Viking

VIKING

Published by the Penguin Group

Penguin Books USA Inc., 375 Hudson Street, New York, New York 10014, U.S.A.

Penguin Books Ltd, 27 Wrights Lane, London W8 5TZ, England

Penguin Books Australia Ltd, Ringwood, Victoria, Australia

Penguin Books Canada Ltd, 10 Alcorn Avenue, Toronto, Ontario, Canada M4V 3B2

Penguin Books (N.Z.) Ltd, 182–190 Wairau Road, Auckland 10, New Zealand

Penguin Books Ltd, Registered Offices: Harmondsworth, Middlesex, England

Text copyright © David A. Adler, 1980

Illustrations copyright © Susanna Natti, 1980

All rights reserved

First published in 1980 by Viking Penguin Inc.

Published simultaneously in Canada

Printed in U.S.A.

5 7 9 10 8 6

Library of Congress Cataloging in Publication Data

Adler, David A.   Cam Jansen and the mystery of the U.F.O.

(Cam Jansen adventure series; v. 2)

Summary: Ten-year-old Cam, possessor of a photographic memory, and her friend Eric
investigate what seems to be a brief appearance of U.F.O.'s.

[1. Mystery and detective stories]   I. Natti, Susanna.

II. Title.   III. Series: Adler, David A.   Cam Jansen adventure series; v. 2.

PZ7.A2615Cao   1980   [Fic]   80-15580   ISBN 0-670-20041-7

For my brother Eddie.
He always made us proud.

Cam Jansen and the
Mystery of the U.F.O.

Chapter One

One cold November afternoon Cam Jansen and her friend Eric Shelton were walking through town. Eric wanted to enter a photography contest. Cam was helping him look for something to photograph.

Cam picked up a crumpled potato chip bag from the street and held it over a litter basket.

"Take my picture," she said. "You can call it 'Local Girl Cleans Up.'"

"I can't take a posed picture," Eric told her. "You know the rules."

3

Eric reached into his pocket and took out a page torn from a newspaper.

"Here it is," Eric said, pointing to the page, "rule three."

"I know the rules," Cam said.

Cam closed her eyes and said, *"Click."* She always said, *"Click,"* when she wanted to remember something. "My mind is a mental camera," Cam often explained, "and cameras go *click.*

"Announcing our first Junior News Photography Contest," Cam said. Her eyes were still closed. "Grand prize one hundred dollars. Entry rules. One. Only twelve-year-olds and under may enter."

As Cam talked, Eric looked at the contest announcement in the newspaper.

"Two. Photographs must be black-and-white. Three. Photographs must be of local interest. They must not be posed. Four. All entries must be received no later than November thirtieth."

"You did it!" Eric said. "You got every word right!"

People said Cam had a photographic memory. They meant Cam could remember an entire scene. When Cam wanted to remember something, even a detail such as how many buttons were on someone's coat, she just looked at the photograph stored in her brain.

Cam's real name is Jennifer. But people started calling her "The Camera" because of her photographic memory and because she said, *"Click,"* so often. Soon "The Camera" was shortened to "Cam."

"Now check me," Cam said. Her eyes were still closed. "I'm going to say the rules backwards.

"Thirtieth—November—than—later— no—received—be—must—entries—all— four—posed—be . . ."

"Enough! Enough!" Eric said. "You're going too fast. I can't keep up."

Cam opened her eyes.

"How did you do that?" Eric asked.

"I have a picture of the rules in my mind. I just read from it."

Cam put her books and lunch box down. "It's cold," she said.

Cam closed the top button of her coat. She pulled down the knitted cap she was wearing until it covered the tops of her ears.

"And it's getting dark," Eric said. "I'm not going to find anything to photograph now. Let's go home."

Eric put the camera back in its case. "I'm never around when anything happens," he complained. "And I'll bet if I am around, either I won't have my camera or I'll be out of film."

"Or," Cam said, "you'll forget to take the lens cap off."

Cam and Eric often spent time together. They were in the same fifth-grade class and lived next door to each other.

"If it wasn't for your hair," Cam's mother often teased, "I'd think you and Eric were twins."

Cam had what people called bright red hair, even though it was more orange than red. Eric's hair was dark brown.

Cam and Eric started walking home. They walked past a row of small stores at the edge of a shopping mall. Then they stopped at the corner and waited for the traffic light to change.

Meow.

Cam and Eric looked up. A gray-and-white kitten was high in a tree. The branch she was standing on was shaking. The kitten took a step toward the end of the branch. The branch shook even more.

Meow.

"I think she wants to come down," Eric said, "but she doesn't know how."

Cam opened her lunch box. "I have part

of a tuna sandwich in here. Maybe I can get the kitten to come down."

Cam reached up and put a piece of tuna fish on the part of the branch closest to the trunk. The kitten saw the food and turned around carefully. The branch shook, but the kitten didn't fall. She walked down the branch and ate the tuna fish. Cam reached out for the kitten.

Eric was holding his camera. "Smile," he said, and he took a picture just as the kitten jumped into Cam's arms.

"I'll call the picture 'Local Girl Saves Untamed Feline.' "

Cam turned to put the kitten down. Then she stopped. She heard noises. Across the street people were shouting and pointing. Cam looked to see what they were pointing at.

In the distance Cam and Eric saw floating green, yellow, blue, and red lights. The lights seemed to brush against one of the trees at the edge of the park. Cam looked straight at the lights and said, *"Click."*

Chapter Two

Eric aimed his camera at the lights. He pressed the shutter button, and the camera went *click*.

The lights were rising, but they weren't going straight up. They were moving from side to side and up and down. It almost seemed that the wind was moving the lights.

Eric aimed his camera again. He pressed the shutter button. *Click*. He pressed it once more. *Click*.

"I'm not sure I'm doing this right," Eric

said. "It's getting dark, and the lights are so far away. I hope at least one picture comes out."

Cam wasn't really listening. She was watching the lights.

"I've seen lights in the sky before," she said, "but they were from helicopters or airplanes or fireworks. I don't know what these are."

"Let's go over there," Eric said, pointing to the parking lot. "Maybe those people know."

Cam put the kitten down. Cam was picking up her books when she heard the kitten cry. The kitten was up in the tree again.

"That cat doesn't seem to learn," Cam said.

"The last time she was up there, you fed her some tuna fish," Eric said. "The kitten learned that if she climbs a tree, she gets something to eat."

Cam opened her lunch box. "Well, all I have this time is bread."

Cam reached up and put the bread on the branch. The kitten turned around carefully. She came down the branch and ate the bread.

"I'm going to hold on to you," Cam said as she put the kitten in her coat pocket. "If I don't, you'll just climb that tree again."

Cam and Eric crossed the street. The people in the brightly lit parking lot were all looking up. Some children were taking photographs. A man and a woman were looking through pairs of binoculars.

"Six lights, no, seven," the man said. "Three green lights, two yellow, one blue, and two red. That's eight. I have to get this right if I'm going to write it down."

The man was wearing a big open shoulder bag. A notebook and a book called *Bird Watcher's Guide* were sticking out.

"I've got it!" the man said as he put the binoculars in his bag. "Seven flying lights.

"You said we wouldn't see anything," he told the woman next to him, "but you were wrong. We've seen a red-backed sandpiper, a bufflehead, an old-squaw, and now this."

The woman put her binoculars into a case. "It wasn't a sandpiper," she said. "It was a golden plover. The old-squaw you thought we saw was a pintail. And there are eight lights up there, not seven."

Cam and Eric could hardly see the lights now. They were just tiny dots of color.

"Can I look through those?" Cam asked the woman.

The woman took the binoculars out of the case and handed them to Cam.

Cam could see why the couple had trouble counting the lights. Sometimes one would move one way, while another moved in a different direction. Sometimes one light moved behind the others and could not be seen at all. Cam also saw lines, like thin wires, pointing down from each light.

Cam looked straight at the lights and said, "*Click*."

"Let me see," Eric said.

"Just a minute."

The lights were floating up. Cam looked carefully at just one light, a blue one. At

first Cam thought it was round, but it wasn't. It was shaped like an egg with a point at the bottom. Cam looked straight at the light and said, *"Click."* Then the lights floated into a cloud and Cam couldn't see them any more.

"They're gone," Cam told Eric. Then she returned the binoculars to the woman.

"Are there seven lights up there or eight?" the woman asked.

"Ah, I'm not sure. The lights keep moving and disappearing. They're hard to count."

"Well, there are eight," the woman said. "I'm sure."

Eric pulled on Cam's sleeve. "I have one picture left. What should it be?"

Cam was going to tell Eric to photograph the crowd, but Eric yelled, "I've got it! Don't move."

Eric bent down and took a picture of the kitten. She was leaning out of Cam's

pocket and eating from someone's bag of groceries.

Cam pulled away. The kitten fell back into her pocket. Some food was still in the kitten's mouth.

"Well, that's it," Eric said. "I hope nothing else happens. I'm out of film."

"Look! Look!" someone in the crowd yelled. "More lights!"

Chapter Three

Cam and Eric turned to look. These lights were not a mystery. A fire department light truck drove up and parked nearby. Several of its large, moving beams of light searched the sky. The mysterious lights were just tiny dots of color. They floated in and out of the clouds.

Then a television news truck drove into the parking lot. A young woman holding a microphone got out of the truck. A man holding a television camera followed her.

The woman walked through the crowd

and asked questions. Then she stood facing the cameraman. She took a deep breath, smiled, and spoke into the microphone.

"This is Stephanie Jackson," she said. "I'm here in the parking lot at the corner of Fillmore and Harrison avenues. Just moments ago these people saw several mysterious lights rise into the night. People here are already calling these lights U.F.O.s—unidentified flying objects."

Cam and Eric moved closer to the reporter to hear what she was saying.

"Many U.F.O.s are later found to be weather balloons, kites, clouds, or even high-flying airplanes. Sometimes they are only pranks meant to fool us.

"Others are never identified. Many people believe that some of the truly unidentified flying objects are aircraft from other planets. Some people even claim to have seen strange creatures get off those flying objects.

"We still don't know what was seen here tonight. We may never know."

Stephanie Jackson turned to a man standing nearby. "Sir, can you tell our viewers what you saw?"

The man took off his hat. With his hand he brushed his hair down. He smiled and spoke into the microphone. "I saw lights," he said in a loud voice.

"Yes, well, maybe this girl can tell us more." The reporter held the microphone in front of Cam. With her free hand the reporter turned Cam to face the camera. "What did you see?" she asked.

Cam closed her eyes. She said, *"Click."*

The people near Cam smiled. A few laughed. *Click* was a strange answer to the reporter's question.

"Well, at first," Cam said, "I thought there was just one U.F.O. But the lights moved apart sometimes, so I think there were a lot of small U.F.O.s flying together.

21

And at one time they were close to the ground. I know that because as they were going up, they touched one of the trees outside the park."

As Cam was speaking, she noticed that Stephanie Jackson was moving away from her. Then Cam saw why. The kitten was leaning out of Cam's coat and licking the reporter's free hand.

"Thank you very much," the reporter said. She walked away quickly.

"But there's more!" Cam said.

"The lights can no longer be seen," the reporter said into the microphone. "They remain a mystery. We don't know what they are or where they came from. But I'm sure the people here tonight will remember what they saw for a long time to come."

The report was over. Stephanie Jackson put the microphone down. She wiped her hand with some tissues. Then she and the

cameraman went back to the truck.

The crowd started to move apart. Some people went to their cars. Others walked across the parking lot to the shopping area.

Cam pulled Eric to a corner of the parking lot. She closed her eyes and said, "*Click*.

"I can't see it!" Cam said. "Come on, Eric. Let's cross the street."

Cam and Eric waited at the corner for the light to change.

"What can't you see?" Eric asked.

"The tree. When the U.F.O.s went up, they hit a tree. I can't see which one it was."

The light changed. Cam and Eric crossed the street.

"The reporter said that some people have seen U.F.O.s land," Cam told Eric. "Creatures from outer space got out. Well, these U.F.O.s hit a tree. They might have landed near the tree."

Cam stood at the corner. She faced the park. "This is where I first saw the U.F.O.s," Cam said. "Sometimes, if I stand where I first saw something, it helps me remember."

Cam closed her eyes. She said, "*Click*."

Then she said, "I see it! It's a small tree between two evergreens. Come on, Eric. Let's go there and take a look. Maybe the U.F.O.s left something behind."

"Something," Eric said, "or someone."

Chapter Four

Cam and Eric were a long way from the park. It was past five o'clock and already quite dark.

"Let's go," Eric said. "It's late. My parents are going out. I have to baby-sit for Howie and the twins tonight. And besides," Eric went on, "we have homework to do. We can come back tomorrow when it's light out."

"Don't worry." Cam told him. "As soon as we've seen what's on the other side of that tree, we'll go home."

Cam felt something moving in her coat pocket. The flap opened and the kitten looked out. Cam petted the back of the kitten's neck. The kitten purred. The flap closed as she settled back into the warmth of Cam's pocket.

"I think you've got yourself a pet," Eric said. "Let's give her a name."

"She likes to climb trees," Cam said as they walked along. "We could call her Twigs or Leaves." Cam thought for a minute. "Or we could give her an outer-space name. After all, we found her and saw a U.F.O. at the same time."

"Well," Eric said, "we can call her Rocket or Stars or Saturn."

"Saturn, that's good," said Cam. "We'll name her after one of the planets. Let's see. There's Mars and Pluto and Neptune. That's a good name for a cat. We'll call her Neptune."

Cam and Eric were getting close to the

park. Cam stopped and looked at the trees.

There were many different evergreens. Evergreens are green all year and are easy to tell apart. But the other trees, the ones without leaves, all looked the same.

Cam closed her eyes. She said, "*Click*. The tree the U.F.O.s hit has white bark. It's a birch between two tall pines."

Cam opened her eyes. "That's the one," she said, pointing.

Cam and Eric walked past the birch tree. The park was empty and dark. The only light came from street lamps outside.

Cam and Eric looked for some hint of a U.F.O. landing. There was nothing near the tree. Toward the center of the park Eric found two ripped balloons.

"Here's something," Cam said. She held up the wrappings from several small pocket flashlights, and a used roll of tape. "But these aren't from outer space."

Cam and Eric kept looking. The ground was covered with leaves. They found cigarette butts, crushed soda cans, and candy-bar wrappers.

Then Cam and Eric heard noises. It sounded like people talking, but they couldn't make out the words. A motor started and bright lights went on. The lights were behind the wall of the handball court.

"Let's see what's over there," Cam whispered.

"No. Let's go back. We have homework."

"We can do it later. Come on."

Cam walked carefully through the leaves. She tried not to make any noise. Eric followed her.

"Look!" Eric said.

A strange-looking creature with wrinkled silver skin ran out. It had a head, arms, and legs and was about the same height as Cam and Eric. Its hands were green and its

feet were blue. It was holding something long and thin.

Then a second creature ran out. It was carrying a pile of colored objects. Both creatures dropped what they were holding and ran back behind the wall.

Chapter Five

Cam and Eric stood still. They were afraid
to move.

"What do we do now?" Eric whispered.

"I don't know. Let's just wait."

Cam and Eric waited quietly. They saw
one of the creatures run out again. It was
holding something.

"Get back here, Cindy," a voice called
out. The silver creature dropped what it
was holding and ran back behind the wall.

"Did you hear that!" Cam said. "They
speak English. Now how would a creature

from outer space learn English?"

"Well, maybe they studied it in school," Eric said. "Or maybe they've been here before." Eric thought for a minute. "Or maybe they're wondering how come we speak *their* language."

"Or maybe they're not from outer space," Cam said. "Come on. Let's get closer."

Eric didn't want to get closer. He wanted to go home. But before he could tell Cam, she ran ahead.

She ran from one tree to the next. Eric followed her. They tried to run quietly, but the dried leaves made noise when Cam and Eric stepped on them. Neptune made noise, too. She meowed inside Cam's pocket.

Cam and Eric stopped running when they reached a large tree close to the wall of the handball court. There was a pile of leaves next to the tree. Cam put her lunch box and books down. She tried to hide behind the leaves. She couldn't. The pile was too small.

"Help me," she whispered to Eric. "Let's build this up."

Eric passed leaves to Cam and she placed them on top of the pile. When the pile was high enough, Cam and Eric crawled behind it.

They waited. They watched the wall, but nothing happened. It was quiet.

Cam took Neptune out of her pocket. She stroked the back of her neck. Neptune purred softly.

"If we could see what they dropped behind that wall," Cam said, "we might be able to find out who they are."

Cam put Neptune back in her pocket. Cam crawled around the tree. She got closer to the wall. Then Cam stopped. She heard voices on the other side of the wall.

"Cindy," a boy's voice said, "fold your arms like this. And, Steven, you stand like this."

There was a flash of light on the other side of the wall.

"Steven, you hold the ray gun. Cindy, you sit down next to Steven."

"Oh, Bobby, why can't *I* hold the ray gun?"

Cam crawled closer. She could see a pile of colored objects ahead, behind the wall.

"Don't smile," Cam heard Bobby say. "Look curious."

There was another flash of light.

Cam crawled closer to the wall. The pile of colored objects were children's sneakers, two jackets, an empty box of aluminum foil, and the wrappings from two pairs of green rubber gloves.

Sneakers? Cam thought. *Aluminum foil and rubber gloves?*

Cam sat there. She looked at the sneakers and the coats. *These aren't creatures*

from outer space, Cam told herself. *They're children covered with aluminum foil.*

Cam reached into her pocket. Neptune was still there. She licked Cam's hand and purred.

Then Cam looked back at Eric. He was signaling for Cam to come back. She didn't. She crawled along the back of the wall. There was a large tree just at the edge of the wall. Cam hid behind it and looked out.

A car was parked facing the handball court. Its headlights were on. There were two children covered with aluminum foil. They were both wearing blue wool socks and green rubber gloves. One was holding a toy ray gun. The children's faces were hidden behind silver masks with holes for their eyes and mouths. An older boy, the one called Bobby, was there, too. He was about eighteen. He had a camera and was taking pictures.

It was hard for Cam to see the children and the older boy clearly. The lights from the car reflected off the aluminum foil. Cam held her hand over her eyes to shield them. She looked straight at the two children and said, "*Click*."

Cam heard a noise behind her. Then she felt something poke her in the back.

Cam was afraid to move.

Chapter Six

Without turning around, Cam reached behind her. Something thin and pointed poked her hand. Slowly Cam turned around. It was Eric. He had moved closer to the wall. He was hiding behind a big tree and was trying to get Cam's attention by poking her with a branch.

Cam crawled back to join him. The tree was almost wide enough to hide them both. When Cam looked out, she could clearly see the front of the handball court.

"You were right," Eric said. "They're not from outer space."

Cam and Eric watched while Bobby took photographs. "Bend down," Bobby told Cindy, "like you're looking at something."

"I can't bend. This foil is too tight. Let Steven bend."

Steven crouched down and picked up a leaf. The foil covering his knees ripped. His pants showed through.

"See," Cindy said. "I told you!"

"All right," Bobby said, "hold this newspaper. Hold it like you don't know what it is."

Cindy held the newspaper upside down. Steven put a page into his mouth as if he were trying to eat it.

"Good, very good," Bobby said as he took another picture.

"You know what," Eric whispered to Cam. "I'll bet he's planning to enter the photography contest and win the hundred dollars."

Bobby continued to take photographs.

"No one will believe him," Eric went on. "No one will believe that creatures from outer space landed."

"We almost believed it," Cam said. "After we saw those U.F.O.s take off, we were ready to believe it."

Cam sat behind the tree with her legs crossed and thought. While she sat there,

Neptune crawled out of Cam's pocket and into her lap.

"But how could they have known," Cam asked, "that we would see a U.F.O. tonight?" Cam thought for a minute. "Unless," she said, "the U.F.O.s were a prank and they're the ones who did it."

Eric looked at the handball court.

"They're taking off their masks. What do we do now?"

Cam jumped up. Neptune fell off her lap and ran away.

"Quick!" Cam said. "Take their pictures while they have their costumes half on and half off. A picture like that would prove they're fakes."

Eric held his camera up and looked through it. He pressed the shutter. Nothing happened. Eric pressed it again. Again nothing.

Eric looked at the back of the camera. "Oh, no!" he said. "I'm out of film. I took

the last picture in the parking lot."

Eric opened his camera. He took out the roll of film and put it in his pocket.

"Let's go back," Eric said, "and get someone to help."

Just as Cam and Eric were leaving, they heard Neptune.

Meow.

Neptune was standing on a branch that hung right over the handball court. The branch was shaking.

"Neptune's going to fall," Eric said, "and right on top of Bobby!"

Chapter Seven

M*eow*.

Neptune raised her right paw. The branch shook.

Neptune fell. She fell right onto Bobby's shoulder. Then Neptune jumped into a pile of aluminum foil. She grabbed a silver mask in her mouth and ran off.

"Get that cat!" Bobby yelled. "Get that mask!"

Bobby dropped his camera and ran after Neptune. Steven and Cindy followed. They chased Neptune around the car, over low

46

bushes, and between trees. They couldn't
keep up with Neptune.

But Neptune wasn't running away. She
was playing a game. When she saw the
others were far behind, she turned around
and ran toward them. She ran close and
then darted away.

Then Neptune ran to Cam and Eric.

"Quick, let's hide," Eric said. He dived
into a pile of leaves.

"No!" Cam yelled. "Let's run."

Cam started to run. She didn't get far.
Steven and Cindy caught her. Bobby
reached into the pile of leaves and pulled
Eric out.

"Look what I found," Bobby said, "a walking tree."

Eric shook the leaves off.

Neptune stopped running. She sat next to Cam and purred. Steven took the mask out of Neptune's mouth.

"What are you doing here?" Bobby asked.

"Watching you," Cam said. "We know Steven and Cindy aren't from another planet."

"No one will believe you took photographs of creatures from another world," Eric said. "And anyway, you can't enter the contest because you're too old."

Bobby laughed.

"I'm entering for him," Cindy said.

"And I'm not worried," Bobby said. "They'll believe me. If they believed that some balloons and flashlights could be a U.F.O., they'll believe creatures from outer space got off and looked around."

48

"Well," Eric said, "we saw you. We'll tell about what you did."

Bobby laughed again. "Oh, no, you won't. If you don't tell anyone what you saw, we'll share the prize money with you."

"We don't need a share," Cam said. "We'll win the whole hundred dollars by ourselves."

Eric looked at Cam. He didn't know what she was talking about.

"We have pictures of Steven and Cindy with their costumes half off," Cam said. "That proves this whole thing is a fake."

"Give me that!" Bobby said. He grabbed Eric's camera.

While Bobby was opening the camera, Cam reached into Eric's pocket. She took the film out and put it in Neptune's mouth. "Run!" she yelled.

Neptune ran off.

"The cat's got the film," Steven said.

"Get it!" Bobby told Steven and Cindy. "I'll follow in the car."

Steven and Cindy ran after Neptune. Bobby got into the car. He left his camera and camera bag behind. He backed up the car.

Crunch.

The car ran over the camera. Then it went forward and out of the park.

Cam ran over to the broken camera.

"Look," she said. "Their film is ruined. Now they can't enter the contest."

Cam gathered her books and lunch box. Eric closed his camera, put it back into the case, and picked up his books. They walked out of the park.

"I'm glad they can't enter the contest," Eric said. "But it's too bad we lost Neptune."

"Maybe not," Cam said. "There's one place we can look, and it's on the way home.

"I should have known," Cam said as they walked. "The lights were shaped like balloons. Bobby must have taped tiny flashlights to them. That's what made them look like colored lights."

"But how could he be sure the balloons would go up?" Eric asked.

"They were probably filled with helium, like the balloons they sell in the zoo.

"It was dark," Cam went on. "No one was near the park so no one knew what the lights were."

Cam led Eric back to the tree where they first found Neptune.

Meow.

There was Neptune, resting on one of the branches. On the ground right under the branch was Eric's roll of film. He picked it up.

When Neptune saw Cam and Eric, she moved toward the end of the branch. The branch began to shake.

Meow.

Cam held out her arms. "You're not getting any food," she said, "so you might as well come down."

Neptune jumped into Cam's arms, looked up at her, and purred. Cam put Neptune in her coat pocket, picked up her books and lunch box, and started to walk home with Eric.

Cam smiled. "Now," she said to Eric, "we can go home and do our homework."

Chapter Eight

Three weeks later Cam was at Eric's house. They were watching the evening news on television. Cam was sitting on the floor holding Neptune. Eric was sitting on the couch. His baby brother, Howie, was in his arms drinking from a bottle.

"And now," the television reporter said, "let's go to Stephanie Jackson, who is standing by."

Stephanie Jackson's picture came on the television screen. "The winners in the Junior News Photography Contest have just been announced," she said.

"This is it!" Cam said.

Stephanie Jackson held up a photograph of a window washer. He was cleaning the windows of one of the city's tallest buildings. A bird had landed on his head.

"This is the winning photograph. It was taken by eleven-year-old Karen Grey."

Stephanie Jackson held up two other photographs. The first was of a crowd of people watching the U.F.O.s.

The second photograph was of Neptune. Neptune was leaning out of Cam's pocket and was eating from someone's bag of groceries.

"These two photographs were awarded honorable mention. One was taken by twelve-year-old Michael Wagner. The other was taken by ten-year-old Eric Shelton. Congratulations."

"I won! I won!" Eric shouted.

Cam smiled. "We always talk about my amazing mental camera," she said, "but I think you. and your camera are pretty amazing, too."

CAM JANSEN

and the
Mystery of the
Dinosaur Bones

★ ★

DAVID A. ADLER
Illustrated by Susanna Natti

★ ★

Viking

VIKING
A Division of Penguin Books USA Inc.,
375 Hudson Street, New York, New York 10014
Penguin Books Ltd, 27 Wrights Lane, London W8 5TZ, England
Penguin Books Australia Ltd, Ringwood, Victoria, Australia
Penguin Books Canada Ltd, 10 Alcorn Avenue, Toronto, Ontario, Canada M4V 3B2
Penguin Books (N.Z.) Ltd, 182–190 Wairau Road, Auckland 10, New Zealand

Penguin Books Ltd, Registered Offices: Harmondsworth, Middlesex, England

Text copyright © David A. Adler, 1981
Illustrations copyright © Susanna Natti, 1981
All rights reserved
First published in 1981 by Viking Penguin Inc.
Published simultaneously in Canada
Printed in the United States of America
Set in Baskerville

Library of Congress Cataloging in Publication Data
Adler, David A.
Cam Jansen and the mystery of the dinosaur bones.
(The Cam Jansen adventure series; v. 3)
Summary: When she notices some bones missing from
a dinosaur skeleton exhibited in the museum, a young
girl with a photographic memory tries to discover who
has been taking them and why.
[1. Mystery and detective stories] I. Natti,
Susanna.   II. Title   III. Series.
PZ7.A2615Cal   [Fic]   80-25132   ISBN 0-670-20040-9

To two wonderful people,
my parents

Chapter One

"*Slurp.*"

Cam Jansen was drinking milk through a straw. She tilted the container to get the last few drops.

Cam was eating lunch in the cafeteria of the Kurt Daub Museum. She was there with her fifth-grade class. Her friend Eric Shelton was sitting next to her.

Cam pointed to the teacher. The teacher was standing on a chair with a finger over her mouth.

1

"Look," Cam said to Eric. "Ms. Benson is waiting for us to be quiet."

"Our tour will begin in twenty minutes," Ms. Benson said. "But first I must ask those of you who brought cameras along to keep your cameras in their cases. The

taking of photographs in the museum is not allowed."

Ms. Benson got down from the chair.

"See," Cam said to Eric, "I told you not to bring your camera. Last time I was here someone was told to leave the museum because he was taking pictures."

"Well," Eric said, "maybe I can't take pictures, but you can. Take a picture of me now with your mental camera."

Cam's mental camera is her memory. She can take one look at a page in a book, close her eyes, and remember every word on the page. "It's easy for me," Cam often explained. "I have a photograph of the page stored in my brain. When I want to remember what I saw, I just look at the photograph."

When people found out about Cam's amazing photographic memory, they stopped using her real name, Jennifer. They started calling her "The Camera."

Soon "The Camera" was shortened to "Cam."

Cam looked straight at Eric and said, *"Click."* She always said, *"Click,"* when she wanted to remember something. Cam says that *"Click"* is the sound her mental camera makes when it takes a picture.

"Close your eyes," Eric said. "Now what do you remember?"

Cam thought for a moment. Then she said, "There's a drop of mustard on your collar. You should wipe it off!"

Eric looked down. There *was* a drop of mustard on his collar. He took a napkin and wiped it off.

"On the side of the milk container you just bought," Cam went on, "it says, 'Edna's. Our cows send you their love and their milk.'

"You're wearing a blue shirt. The top button of the shirt once came off and someone sewed it back on."

4

"You're right," Eric said. "But how did you know about the button?"

Cam opened her eyes. "It's the thread," she said. "I remembered that the top button was sewn on with white thread. The other buttons have light blue thread."

Ms. Benson was standing on a chair again. She said to the class, "Clean your tables and then get into a double line."

Cam and Eric quickly threw away the empty milk containers and the wrappings from their lunches. Then they got in line.

Ms. Benson led the class up the stairs to the museum lobby. They were met there by a young woman in a purple dress.

"I'm Janet Tyler," the woman in the purple dress said. "I will be your guide. Please stay together and follow me."

The guide led the class to the Air Travel room. She pointed out the models of the earliest flying machines. There was a full-size model of the 1903 Wright brothers' airplane.

Ms. Tyler took the class to a weather station room with a solar energy exhibit. Then she led the class into a large room with a very high ceiling.

"This next exhibit is my favorite," the guide told the class.

"Mine, too," Cam whispered to Eric.

Chapter Two

The class followed the guide into the room. Glass cases filled with old tools, bones, rocks, and photographs lined the walls. On a platform, in the center of the room, was part of the skeleton of a very large dinosaur, the Brachiosaurus. Some of the bones from the skeleton were lying on the platform. The wires had come loose and the skeleton was being repaired.

"This is the skeleton of a Brachiosaurus. Brake-e-o-sawr-us," Janet Tyler said again slowly so everyone could hear how the word was pronounced. "The Brachio-saurus was the biggest dinosaur. It weighed over fifty tons. That's more, I'm sure, than all the children in your whole school weigh together."

Then the guide led the class to another dinosaur skeleton. It was much smaller than the Brachiosaurus. Its mouth was open and its hands were stretched out as if it were ready to grab something to eat.

"Look at those teeth," someone in the class said.

"And look at that tail. It's so long and pointy."

"This is the skeleton of a Coelophysis," the guide said. "Seel-o-fy-sis," she said again slowly. "Now you may know about some dinosaurs, but I'm sure no one knows anything about the Coelophysis."

"I do," Cam said.

Everyone turned to look at Cam. They were surprised that she knew about the

Coelophysis. Ms. Benson had never mentioned it when she taught the class about dinosaurs.

Cam had read about the Coelophysis. She wanted to remember exactly what the book said. She closed her eyes and said, *"Click."*

When Cam said, *"Click,"* the guide started to laugh. She covered her mouth with her hand.

"The Coelophysis," Cam said with her eyes still closed, "was one of the first dinosaurs. It was about eight feet long, including its tail. It weighed no more than fifty pounds. It was a meat eater and . . ."

"Yes, thank you," the guide said before Cam had a chance to finish. "What you may not know is that these bones were discovered by Dr. Kurt Daub, the scientist who started this museum."

"Are people still finding dinosaur bones?" Eric asked.

"Yes," Ms. Tyler answered. "I'll be going on a dinosaur hunt in a few weeks, and I hope to find some myself."

Someone else asked, "Are all those bones real?"

"No. Dr. Daub didn't find a complete skeleton. Some of these bones were made from plaster of Paris."

There were many other questions, but Cam stopped listening. She was busy studying the dinosaur's tail.

"Something is wrong," she whispered to Eric.

Cam closed her eyes and said, *"Click."* She kept them closed for a while. Then she

looked again at the dinosaur's tail.

"I was right," Cam said to Eric. "Something *is* wrong. Three of the dinosaur's bones are missing."

Chapter Three

Cam raised her hand and tried to get the museum guide's attention. But Ms. Tyler looked past her.

The guide pointed to a boy wearing a suit and a bow tie. "You have a question."

"I want to know why they are called dinosaurs."

Ms. Tyler smiled. "The name 'dinosaur' comes from two words, 'dino' which means 'terrible,' and 'saur' which means 'lizard.' So when we call them dinosaurs, we are really calling them terrible lizards."

"What did dinosaurs eat?" another boy asked.

"Some ate meat. Some ate plants, and some ate the eggs of other dinosaurs."

Then the guide looked at Cam. She smiled. "It seems that the red-haired girl, the one who says, *'Click,'* has a question."

"What happened to the tail?" Cam asked. "The last time I was here, it had three more bones. They were right here."

Cam pointed to the part of the tail near the hip. Farther down, there were bones that hung down from the tail like ribs. Where Cam pointed there weren't any bones.

"There's nothing missing on this dinosaur," the guide said quickly. "Now, are there any other questions?"

"But there *are* some bones missing. I've been here before and—"

"I'm here every day, and this skeleton

16

looks the same as it always does."

The guide answered a few other questions. Then she told Ms. Benson that the tour was finished, and she walked away.

Ms. Benson was a short woman. She stood on her toes so the whole class could see her.

"It's still early," Ms. Benson said. "You

have an hour to go through the museum by yourselves. At two-thirty all of you must be in the front lobby. If you don't have a watch, please stay near someone who does."

"Let's go to the gift shop," Eric said to Cam. "I want to buy presents for my twin sisters and my brother, Howie."

In the gift shop there were shelves of books and racks of postcards. Kits to make airplane models and models of dinosaurs were piled on a table with toys and games.

"All I have is a dollar," Eric said. "I hope I can find something."

While Eric looked around, Cam opened a big book called *Dinosaurs*. There was a whole page on the Coelophysis, but there was no illustration of its skeleton. The book told about how the Coelophysis hunted for food and how it might have looked, but it did not say how many bones the Coelophysis had in its tail.

"Look what I bought for the twins," Eric said a few minutes later. He reached into a bag and took out two small whistles, each in the shape of a Brachiosaurus. Cam took one of the whistles and blew into it. It was a dog whistle. It made a sound dogs could hear clearly, but Cam and Eric could hardly hear it.

"These whistles are for calling dogs," Cam said. "Why did you buy them? Your family doesn't have a dog."

"I know, but these whistles are also toy dinosaurs, and they're just twenty-nine cents each. Everything else costs too much."

Eric reached into the bag again and took out two postcards. "Look at these," he said. "This one is for Howie." It was a picture of a hot-air balloon. "And this one is for me." The second postcard had a picture of the Coelophysis skeleton.

"Let me see that," Cam said.

Cam looked at the postcard carefully. Then she closed her eyes and said, *"Click."*

"This is it!" she said, waving the postcard. "This is the way the skeleton looked when I saw it the last time I was here. Let's go to the dinosaur room. You'll see. Some bones are missing."

Cam and Eric quickly walked through the museum.

"All right," Cam said when they stood in front of the Coelophysis skeleton. "You count the bones hanging from the tail of the skeleton. I'll count the ones on the postcard."

Cam counted the bones on the postcard a few times. Then she said, "I counted thirty-four on the tail. How many did you count?"

"Thirty-one."

Chapter Four

Cam looked at her watch. It was two-thirty.

"Come on, Eric," she said. "It's time to go."

Eric put the postcards and whistles in his pocket, and they went to meet the class in the lobby. Ms. Benson asked the class to line up. Then she led them to the school bus.

On the bus Cam and Eric talked about the missing dinosaur bones.

"Why would anyone want them?" Eric asked.

"And how could anyone steal the bones?" Cam added. "The skeleton is wired together. In the time it would take to unhook a bone, I'm sure someone would walk by and see what they were doing."

The bus stopped in the school parking lot. Ms. Benson stood up.

"It's after three o'clock," she said. "So you may all go home."

It was a warm spring day. Cam and Eric had ridden their bicycles to school that morning. They went to the rack behind the school to get their bicycles.

As Cam unlocked her bicycle, she said, "The bones can't be taken when the museum is open. There are too many people around then, and too many guards. It must be done after the museum closes. Let's go back there. Maybe we can find out what's going on."

"But the museum closes early today," Eric said. "We won't have any time to look around."

Cam put rubber bands over the cuffs of her pants to keep them from getting caught in the bicycle as she rode.

"All we have to look for is a place to hide," Cam said. "We don't have to be home until six today. We can stay in the dinosaur room after the museum closes and watch to see what happens."

Cam was already on her bicycle. She started to ride away before Eric could tell her that he didn't want to hide in the museum.

Eric got on his bicycle. He pedaled hard, but he couldn't catch up with Cam. By the time he locked his bicycle in front of the museum, Cam was halfway up the steps. He caught up with her in the dinosaur room.

A bell sounded.

"The museum closes in five minutes," a guard called out.

"Let's leave now," Eric said, "or we'll be locked inside."

Cam crawled under a glass case filled with photographs. Eric followed her.

Cam whispered to Eric, "You can leave if you want to, but I'm staying."

The bell sounded again.

From their hiding place Cam and Eric could see only the bottoms of the other exhibit cases and the feet of the dinosaur skeletons. A few people walked past the glass case, but all Cam and Eric could see were their legs. Then it was quiet.

"We did it," Cam said.

It was quiet for a while. But soon Cam and Eric heard footsteps. A man was walking from one case to the next. He stopped at Cam and Eric's case. Then he bent down and looked straight at Cam and Eric.

Chapter Five

It was one of the museum guards.

"Come with me," he said.

The guard led them out of the dinosaur room, through the museum lobby, to the office of the museum director. The guard knocked on the door and walked in. Cam and Eric followed him.

The walls of the office were covered with paintings of prehistoric animals. There were statues of famous scientists and large stuffed animals all over the room. Cam and

Eric couldn't find the director among all those paintings and statues.

"Didn't you hear the bell?" the director asked.

Then Cam and Eric saw him. He was sitting between a statue of a woman scientist and two stuffed owls.

"Yes, we heard the bell," Cam said. "But three dinosaur bones are missing. Someone is stealing bones from the tail of the Coelophysis skeleton, and we want to see who it is."

"That's impossible," the director said, stroking his beard. "Nothing is missing. But if you want to watch over the Coelophysis, you can come back tomorrow when the museum opens." Then he said to the guard, "Now please take these children to the door and make sure that this time they leave the museum."

Cam and Eric followed the guard to the front entrance. The guard opened the door with a key and let them out.

"Now what?" Eric asked.

"There's nothing we can do," Cam said. "We can't get back inside, so let's go home."

While Cam and Eric started to unlock their bicycles, a truck rode past them. It backed into the museum driveway. A sign painted on the side of the truck said, "Beth's Milk Tastes Best."

"That's strange," Cam said. "Milk is usually delivered early in the morning, not late in the afternoon."

A man in a white uniform got out of the truck. He was carrying an empty milk box.

"Maybe some of the milk went bad," Eric said, "and he's picking it up."

The milkman knocked on the garage door. The door opened and he went inside. He came out a few minutes later, carrying a large brown bag in the box. He put it in the truck.

"There's probably a whole bunch of containers of sour milk in that bag," Eric said.

Cam and Eric heard the door on the other side of the truck open and someone get inside, but they couldn't see who it was. Then the truck backed up. As the truck passed them, Cam read the sign again.

"There's something else that's strange about that truck," Cam said. She closed her eyes and said, *"Click."*

"The museum doesn't use Beth's milk. It uses Edna's. That's what it said on the milk container you bought in the cafeteria."

31

Cam got on her bicycle. She turned to Eric and said, "That man wasn't picking up sour milk. He was picking up something else. Come on, let's follow the truck."

Chapter Six

The streets were crowded with cars. It was after four o'clock, and many people were driving home from work. Cam stayed on the right-hand side of the street. Eric rode behind her. The milk truck was already a block ahead. Cam and Eric pedaled hard to catch up.

As Cam pedaled, her bicycle made a loud "clicking" sound. The kickstand was loose, and one of the pedals hit it as it went around.

The milk truck made a right turn onto a

side street, but before Cam and Eric could reach the corner, Cam had to stop. The loose kickstand was in the way. It was impossible for Cam to pedal.

Eric got off his bicycle, too. He pushed the kickstand on Cam's bicycle back into place.

Cam said, "Thank you."

"You really need a new one," Eric told her.

Cam and Eric got on their bicycles again. When they reached the corner, they signaled and turned.

Cam looked ahead. A big brown dog was running along the sidewalk. A few cars were parked along the side of the street. But Cam couldn't see the milk truck. She stopped and waited for Eric.

"We've lost it," Cam said.

"Maybe not. I think I see a truck parked in the driveway of one of the houses on the next block. Maybe it's the milk truck."

Eric led Cam to a small brick house with a white wooden fence around it. The milk truck was parked in the driveway. No one was sitting inside the truck.

"They must have gone into the house," Cam said. She leaned her bicycle against the fence. "You stay here and watch for them," she told Eric. "I'll look around in the back."

There was a high window on the side of the garage. As Cam walked past the window, she heard voices. She looked for something to stand on so she could see inside.

Someone tapped her on the back. It was Eric.

"I locked the bicycles to the fence," he said. "I didn't want to wait out there alone."

Cam found an empty wooden milk box behind the house. She put the box right under the window, climbed up, and looked through.

There was a large table inside the garage. A few small bones and some larger ones were on the table. The milk box with the brown bag that they had seen the man put in the truck was there, too. A bag of plaster of Paris was on the floor near some boxes, and metal tubs and a wheelbarrow with a pickax and shovel in it.

"Get down," Eric whispered. "Someone will see you."

"There's no one there," Cam said. "But there is an open door. Maybe it leads into the house. I'll bet that's where they went."

Eric climbed up on the box.

"Look!" Eric said. "The three missing bones are on that table!"

Eric got off the box. He pulled on Cam's sleeve. "Get down," he said. "Let's go back now."

Cam didn't move. She kept looking through the window.

"We can call the museum," Eric said. "We can tell them we found their missing dinosaur bones."

"Someone is coming through the door," Cam said. "It's the Milkman."

Eric quickly climbed onto the box. Cam

and Eric watched the Milkman take the brown bag out of the box. The bag was tied with string. The Milkman tried to untie the knot. He couldn't.

"Why did you tie it so tight?" he called into the house.

"Use the scissors," a woman's voice answered.

The Milkman reached into one of the boxes. He took out a pair of scissors and cut the string.

"I wonder what could be in there," Eric whispered.

"It can't be a bone from the Coelophysis," Cam said quietly. "It's too big."

The Milkman tore open the side of the bag. There was something large and white inside. He took it out and carefully placed it on the table.

"Wow!" Eric said. "Look at the size of that bone."

"It must be from the Brachiosaurus,"

Cam said, "the one they were fixing in the museum."

The Milkman took out a ruler and measured the bone. He took a pad and pencil from his pocket and wrote on the pad. Then he looked at the bag of plaster of Paris.

"We need more plaster," he called into the house.

"Then let's go get it," the woman said.

The Milkman walked through the open door and into the house.

"They'll probably use the plaster of Paris to make a copy of the bone," Cam said. "They'll take the copy to the museum tomorrow and leave it there in place of the real one."

"But how do they get in and out of the museum?" Eric asked.

"And why do they want the bones?" Cam added.

Cam and Eric stopped talking. They heard the front door of the house open and then slam shut.

After a few minutes Cam whispered, "I didn't hear the truck drive away, but they should be gone by now. Let's take a look."

Cam walked quietly. Eric followed her. Cam peeked out past the edge of the garage wall. She saw that the truck was still in the driveway. And she saw something else.

"Our bicycles," Cam said. "What if *they* see them!"

Chapter Seven

"We sure did see your bicycles," a man said.

Cam turned. It was the Milkman. He was standing behind Eric.

"Janet!" the Milkman called.

A woman came out. She was wearing a purple dress. It was Janet Tyler, the museum guide.

"Well, well," she said. "Look who we have here. It's the Click, Click Girl and her friend."

The Milkman put a key into a lock at the side of the garage door. The lock was

42

electric. He turned the key and the door opened.

The Milkman led Cam and Eric into the garage. He pressed a button on the wall. The garage door closed.

Janet Tyler and the Milkman started to argue. She pointed to the dinosaur bones on the table.

"It's all over. We'll have to give these back. And it's your fault. You should have made copies of the three small bones last night. Then these kids wouldn't have followed us."

"I'm not giving anything back. Not yet," the Milkman said. "We'll do just as we planned. We'll take the bones along on our dinosaur hunt. We'll bury them and then dig them up. *Then* we'll give the bones back to the museum."

Janet closed her eyes and said, "I can just see the newspaper headline: 'Janet Tyler discovers buried dinosaur bones and gives them to the museum.' I'll be famous. I'll speak to science groups all over the country. I'll make a fortune."

Cam pulled on Eric's sleeve and whispered, "This is our chance. Janet's eyes are closed. Take out the whistles you bought."

Eric reached into his pocket. He took out the two dog whistles shaped like dinosaurs. Cam took one of them.

"When I tell you to, blow the whistle," Cam whispered. "Blow it as hard as you can."

"Stop whispering," the Milkman said.

Janet opened her eyes. She seemed surprised to be in the garage with Cam, Eric, and the Milkman.

Then the Milkman told Cam and Eric, "Either you agree not to tell anyone about our plan, or we'll call the museum director. We'll put the bones in your bicycle baskets and tell the director you took them and we caught you."

Cam turned to whisper to Eric.

Janet Tyler smiled. "That's right," she said. "You talk it over with your friend."

"Quietly count to three," Cam whispered. "Then blow the whistle."

"One. . ."

Cam quickly turned around. She pressed the garage door button.

"Two. . ."

The garage door opened.

"Three."

Cam and Eric blew the whistles hard.

Janet could hardly hear the sounds the whistles made. But she knew what kind of whistles they were.

"Get the bones!" Janet yelled. "Get the bones before some dog comes and runs off with them."

She opened the door to the house. The Milkman picked up as many of the bones as he could carry.

"Quick, Eric!" Cam said. "Crawl under the table."

Chapter Eight

Cam and Eric crawled under the table and ran out of the garage. A big brown dog and two smaller dogs ran past them toward the garage.

Cam and Eric ran around the milk truck to the bicycles. Eric tried to open the lock. He turned the dial a few times.

"Hurry!" Cam said.

"I can't remember the combination."

Cam closed her eyes. She said, *"Click."* Then she thought for a moment.

Inside the house there was a noise. Someone was coming out.

"It's four, eighteen, thirty-six," Cam said.

Eric turned the knob. The lock opened. Cam and Eric got on their bicycles just as the Milkman ran out of the house.

"Stop!" he yelled.

"Let's go!" Cam said to Eric.

Cam looked both ways. No cars were coming. She quickly rode across the street. Eric followed her.

Just as they got across the street, they heard the door of the milk truck open and shut. The engine started.

Cam pedaled hard. As she pedaled, her bicycle made a loud clicking sound. She tried to keep pedaling, but she couldn't. The kickstand was in the way.

Cam got off her bicycle. Eric stopped, too. He came over to help.

"Hurry. The truck's coming," Cam said.

Eric pushed the kickstand back into place. They both got back on their bicycles.

Cam started pedaling again. The bicycle made a clicking sound, but not as loud as before.

Cam turned quickly and looked behind

her. Eric was pedaling hard. And the milk truck was right behind Eric.

Cam pedaled as hard as she could. The clicking sound became louder again, but Cam kept pedaling. She signaled and turned the corner. Eric followed her.

"Screech!"

"Honk! Honk!"

Cam stopped pedaling and turned to see what was happening. A car had turned the corner right in front of the milk truck. Both the driver of the car and the Milkman had slammed on their brakes.

"This is our chance," Cam told Eric.

Cam and Eric were riding on a busy street now. There were stores on both sides of the street.

Cam saw a narrow path on the side of a candy store. She rode down the path to the back of the store. Eric followed her.

"Good thinking," Eric said once they had stopped their bicycles. "When the Milkman turns the corner, he won't be able to find us."

Cam got off her bicycle. Then she told Eric, "You stay here and watch the bikes. I'm going inside to call the museum."

There was only one telephone in the store. A large man was using it. Cam opened the telephone book and looked for the museum's number.

"Do you have any shirts on sale?" the man was saying into the telephone. "Yes . . . Extra-large . . . I want a sky-blue shirt. But not a rainy day sky-blue. It should be a sunny day sky-blue."

Cam found the museum's number. She looked at it and said, *"Click."* Then she took a coin from her pocket and waited to use the phone.

". . . and I need a green shirt," the man said into the telephone. "But not grass-green. It should be more like a traffic-light green . . ."

Eric came into the store. "I saw the milk truck. It rode right past me. The Milkman and Janet Tyler looked angry, but they didn't see me or the bicycles."

The man said, "Thank you very much." He hung up and left the booth.

Cam said, *"Click,"* to help her remember the museum's number. Then she dialed.

"Hello," Cam said into the telephone. "I'd like to speak to the director."

She waited.

"This is Jennifer Jansen," Cam said. "I'm the girl who was found hiding in the dinosaur room after the museum closed."

Cam told the director about the Milkman, Janet Tyler, and the dinosaur bones. She also told him the name and address of the candy store. "Yes, we'll wait here for you," Cam said, and then she hung up.

"The museum director is coming," Cam told Eric. "He said that after we left, he went to the dinosaur room. He looked at the skeletons and saw that some bones were missing. He said we should wait in front of the store with our bicycles. When he gets here, he'll follow us to the house."

Chapter Nine

Cam and Eric went behind the store to get their bicycles. Eric started turning the dial on the lock.

"Do you remember the combination?" Cam asked.

"Sure, I only forgot the last time because we were in such a hurry."

As Eric was turning the dial, Cam laughed and said, "You know, I don't think any dog would really be interested in those dinosaur bones. They're too old."

Cam and Eric walked their bicycles to the

54

front of the candy store. They waited for the museum director.

Soon a car drove up and stopped in front of the store. The car was just like the museum exhibits—very old. The director was at the wheel. He waved to Cam and Eric. They got on their bicycles. The director followed them in his car to the small brick house with the white wooden fence. The milk truck was in the driveway again.

"This is it," Cam told the director.

"You don't have to worry about the bones," the director said. "Since I know Janet stole them, she can't bury the bones and pretend to discover them. The bones are no good to her any more, so I'm sure she'll give them back without any trouble."

The museum director got out of his car. "Of course, she'll lose her job and I'll have to report her and her friend to the police. But they should have known that could happen when they took the bones."

The museum director shook hands with Cam and Eric. "I want to thank both of you for all your help," he said. "Before you go, you must tell me how you knew that some bones were missing. I pass those skeletons all the time, and I didn't notice anything."

Cam explained, "The last time I was at the museum, I took a picture of the dinosaur skeleton. When I looked at the picture, I knew some bones were missing."

"But our guards don't let anyone take photographs in the museum."

"Cam's camera is different," said Eric. "She doesn't need film or a flash. Cam's camera is her memory."

The director smiled. "Well, we certainly won't stop your memory from taking photographs." He buttoned his jacket, and then he asked, "Can you take one of me?"

Cam laughed. Then she looked straight at the museum director and said, *"Click."*